First Published 2018
Tiny Tree Children's Books (an imprint of Matthew James Publishing Ltd)
Unit 46, Goyt Mill
Marple
Stockport
SK6 7HX
www.tinytreebooks.com

ISBN: 978-1-910265-66-6

Printed by and bound by
Charlesworth Press Limited www.charlesworth.com

I n the middle of a town, within a community called Baker Estates, on a dead-end street called Holmes, there is a narrow brick house. And inside this brick house, lives a fluffy dog, named Sherlock.

On this day, Sherlock was napping in the middle of a large study in front of a fire, when the doorbell rang. As he lifted his head groggily, he heard a familiar voice at the door which shook him from sleep. He jumped to his shaggy feet and made his way to the top of the stairs to investigate.

He could see the bottom of the door standing open and two sets of legs. Lying on the landing with his paws hanging over the edge of the stairs and his head down, he could see the full picture. He saw Mrs. Hudson and Officer L. Strade talking in rapid tones, with the officer holding a newspaper in his hands.

"Well, I have never heard of such a thing," Mrs. Hudson exclaimed. "A big animal from the forest, roaming around this area?"

"We are warning everyone in the estate, Ma'am," said Officer L. Strade. "Just stay inside at night until this has all been resolved. We're sure the creature is very dangerous."

Sherlock listened closely and tilted his head to the side.

"That cannot be right," he thought to himself. "Surely, I would have sensed if something like that was nearby."

Wanting to know more, he rushed down the stairs, grabbed the newspaper out of the Officer's hand and ran out the open door. He continued around the side of the brick house to the backyard, where he took the paper to study the case further.

Looking through the article something struck him as odd about all of the beastly sightings, but he needed to dig a little deeper before his suspicions were confirmed. Leaving his yard, he went to follow the path of the night beast.

First he went to the trees on the edge of Baker Estates. He put his nose to the ground and quickly caught an unfamiliar scent. Looking towards the tree trunks, he saw small clumps of something black here and there. At first he thought it was just moss covering the bark, but moving closer to inspect, he saw it was actually coarse, black fur.

"Interesting," he thought.

Sherlock continued to follow the path of the beast. He used the scent trail and information from the newspaper to track the route of the black creature. He saw paw prints in the mud leading up to each location of a reported sighting, and once again saw coarse fur sticking to fencing and trees along the way.

As he made his way back to his own home, he saw Gladstone basking in the sunshine on his patio, Mycroft standing at attention at the back windows, and little Adler next door barking for him to come and play.

His suspicions had been confirmed by his search, and he knew what he had to do to catch the beast that was terrorizing the area.

That evening, as the sun was beginning to set, Sherlock had Mrs. Hudson serve him his dinner in the garden. She tried to get him to come inside, worried about the beast on the loose.

"You silly, stubborn guy," she said patting his head and setting down his dish. "You come in soon now. We don't want you getting in a tangle with that thing running about."

When she was inside and out of sight, Sherlock pushed the dish into the middle of the yard. He checked to make sure that the back gate was left slightly open and then made his way inside to cozy up by the fire.

Well into the night, when Mrs. Hudson was fast asleep, Sherlock quietly made his way into the study. He settled himself in front of the big window facing the backyard and waited. And he waited.

Even though it would be hard for the beast to escape back through the gate once it closed, Sherlock hoped his trap of a delicious meal would be enough to lure the beast into the backyard.

Just when he thought that the beast was too smart for this simple plan, he saw the gate slowly push open.

A fuzzy black head appeared around the side, peering around the yard. Getting to his feet, Sherlock padded down the stairs and towards the back door.

He simply watched the creature, not wanting to confront it yet just in case it was dangerous. He watched as the black mass moved, almost crawling through the shadows, towards the bowl.

"Well, it's obviously scared," thought Sherlock, "look how it slinks low to the ground, avoiding any light."

He watched, head tilted, as the black animal cautiously lowered it's head to the food bowl. It quickly pulled it's head back up to look around the yard once more, and then bent it's head to rapidly eat the meal that was left there.

Sherlock jumped up and unlocked the door to enter the backyard, stopping to pick up a bone on the way. He paused just outside the door and watched the poor animal licking the dish to get every last drop.

The beast sensed his presence and slowly looked up, their eyes met. The creature's eyes darted from side-to-side looking for an escape route but could find none, because the gate had closed behind it.

Sherlock could tell the animal was in a panic and knew the situation could quickly turn dangerous if it felt trapped. He dropped the bone in his mouth to the ground, slowly backed up, and then laid down a distance from the food bowl. He hoped the beast would understand that he was offering his bone and sense that he was non-threatening.

The black creature seemed to calm a little now, and then walked tentatively over to the delicious bone. It lay down and started gnawing on the gift, watching Sherlock closely out of the corner of its eye.

The two animals stayed on the grass facing one another for much of the night.
Sherlock always relaxed but aware, and the black creature unsure and a little scared.

After a very long while, the beast stood up. Sherlock was fully aware of the movement, but did not raise his head, not wanting to alarm the creature. It inched slowly towards the spot where Sherlock lay and curled itself up beside him.

At the first sign of daylight, Sherlock awoke and lifted his head. The black beast still lay beside him, fast asleep. He carefully stood up and circled to the head of the creature.

"Just as I suspected," he thought, with a head tilt.

At the sound of the back door opening, Sherlock lolloped towards Mrs. Hudson before she could be alarmed by what she saw before her.

"Sherlock! Were you outside all night? What about the beast prowling around," she asked the shaggy dog with her hands raised in exasperation. Then she raised her eyes and saw the huge, black creature laying in her yard.

Not wanting her to scream out, Sherlock jumped up and put his paws on her shoulders, as if to tell her everything was fine. He dropped to the ground, padded back to the beast, and sat beside it, with his tongue hanging out.

Mrs. Hudson saw that Sherlock was at ease with the situation, so she cautiously made her way towards the two, not wanting to startle the unfamiliar animal. When she was close enough, she knelt down in front of them to appear less threatening, and studied the creature. Suddenly she gasped, realizing just what she was looking at. For sitting in front of her was not a dangerous beast at all, but rather a big black dog with matted, dirty, unkempt hair.

"Oh you poor dear," she exclaimed, reaching out her upturned hand.

The dog was hesitant to move at first, but with her soft voice and some encouragement from Sherlock, it stretched out for some gentle head scratching. Once the animal saw that it was in no danger from her, it began wagging its tail and moved closer for more petting.

"You are no beast, are you," she said, giving it a cuddle. "You were just looking for food all this time."

The dog wagged its tail even more and then licked her cheek.

"You must be starving, poor thing. Let's get you some food."

She stood up and headed back towards the house, with Sherlock following. At the door she looked back and saw that it was still sitting in the yard, not moving.

"Well come on then," she called back to it.

Sherlock barked, his voice ringing out like a bell. With that, the black dog got to its feet and ran towards the door to join them.

Inside, while the two dogs were enjoying a nice breakfast, Mrs. Hudson was worrying about what to do with their visitor. Even though it was in a very messy state, someone must be missing the animal. Sherlock could sense her concern and wanted to help. He suddenly remembered that the night before he could see something shiny around the dog's neck through its dense black fur. He stood in front of Mrs. Hudson and shook his head back and forth, making his own collar jingle.

"A tag! Of course," she declared. "Sherlock, you are a genius!"

Mrs. Hudson reached through the thick, dirty fur and found what she was looking for.

Around the beast's neck was a brown leather collar with a metal tag shaped like a bone. The name 'H. Baskerville' with a phone number was engraved upon it.

"I knew someone must be missing a dog as sweet as you," she said, patting the black dog's head.

She dialed the phone number and a serious sounding man answered. He informed Mrs. Hudson that Mr. H. Baskerville no longer lived at that number, and he had left no forwarding address or number. He then hung up on her without another word.

"Well," she said turning around to face the two dogs, "it looks like you'll be staying with us for a while. Should we get you cleaned up?"

Upstairs in the bathroom, Sherlock looked on as Mrs. Hudson shampooed and cleaned the other dog. All the while she was talking in a sweet, quiet voice to soothe the animal's nerves.

Once out of the bathtub, she trimmed and combed through the thick black fur as best she could, still talking in the same soft voice.

"I really wish we knew what to call you, precious one," she said, drying the top of its head. "If you are going to be staying here until we can find your owner, we have to call you something. Don't we Sherlock?"

Sherlock raised his head to look at her and tilted it to the side. Just then he saw the other dog's collar sitting on the bathroom cabinet where Mrs. Hudson had left it. He stood up to walk towards them and nudged the collar on his way, it fell to the floor with a jingle.

"What's this," she asked, looking down at the floor.

When Sherlock had purposely knocked the collar down, the metal tag flipped over revealing more engraving on the back. Picking it up, her eyes widened.

"Watson," she read out the name.

The black dog's tail began to wag quickly, and he jumped up putting his paws on her. Mrs. Hudson laughed at his excitement and Sherlock barked his approval.

"Well, nice to meet you Watson!"

Later that evening the two dogs were lying by the fire in the study. While Watson slept, Sherlock could hear Mrs. Hudson talking on the phone. She was telling someone about their adventurous day, and their plans to try and find Watson's old home. As he listened to her talk, he settled his head down and started to drift off to sleep too. For even though it had been only he and Mrs. Hudson for a long time, he felt comfortable and happy with this new situation. He knew that Watson was actually already home.